KU-270-472

This

Orchard book

belongs to:

_____

_____

KT 2189359 4

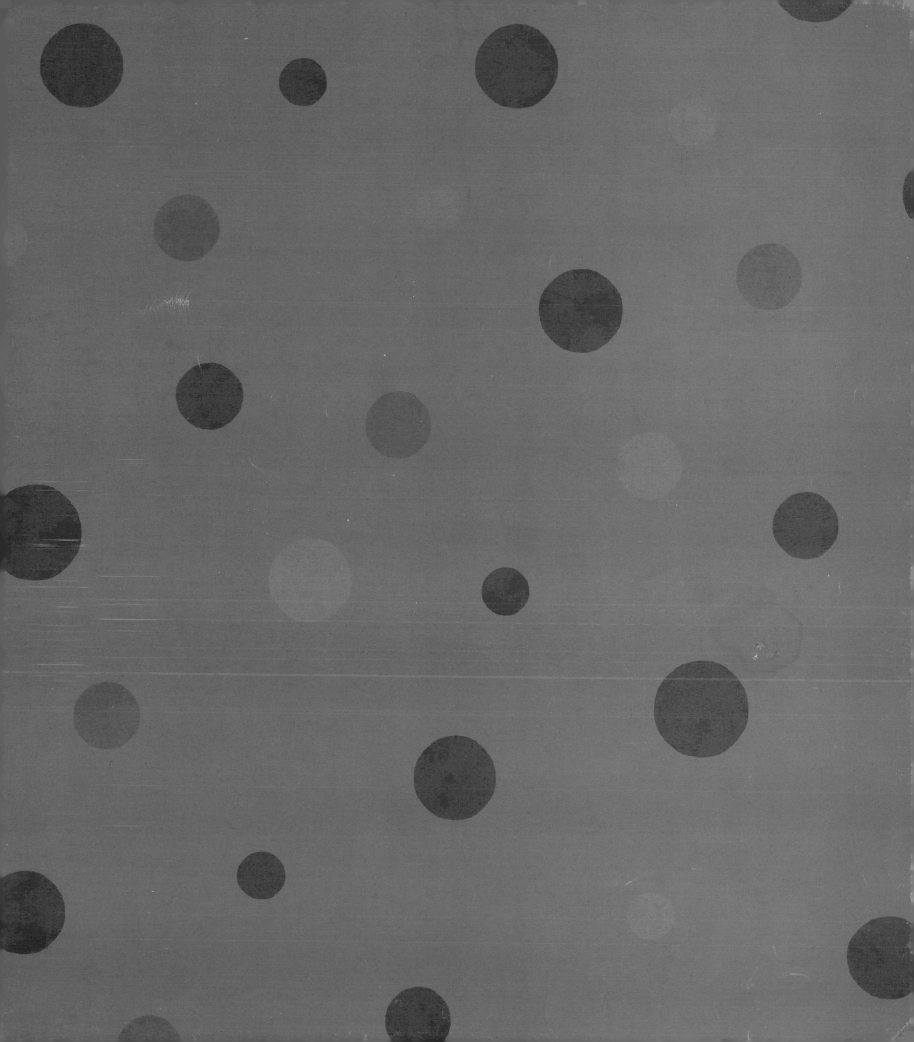

For Talia and Bruno,
with love
Giles

For Leah and Alice
with love from
Emma

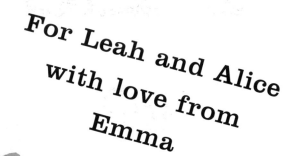

Kingston upon
Thames Libraries

KT 2189359 4	
Askews & Holts	22-Jun-2016
JF JFY	£6.99
S T	KT00001512

ORCHARD BOOKS

338 Euston Road, London NW1 3BH

Orchard Books Australia

Level 17/207 Kent Street, Sydney, NSW 2000

First published in 2013 by Orchard Books

First published in paperback in 2013

ISBN 978 1 40832 433 2

Text © Giles Andreae 2013

Illustrations © Emma Dodd 2013

The rights of Giles Andreae to be identified as the author

and of Emma Dodd to be identified as the illustrator

of this work have been asserted by them in accordance

with the Copyright, Designs and Patents Act, 1988.

A CIP catalogue record for this book

is available from the British Library.

1 3 5 7 9 10 8 6 4 2

Printed in China

Orchard Books is a division

of Hachette Children's Books,

an Hachette UK Company.

www.hachette.co.uk

I Love You

Giles Andreae & Emma Dodd

ORCHARD

I love you, birdies,

singing in the trees.

I love you, butterflies

and little buzzy bees!

I love you, Mummy,

Times a million and a half.

I love you, Daddy,

You really make me laugh!

I love you, doggies, with your funny waggy tails.

I love you, beetles and bugs and snails.

I love you, crabbies, in the pools by the sea.

I love you, fishes – one, two, three!

I love you, best friends . . .

. . . every single one.

Isn't it great to have **such fun!**

I love you, sausages, sizzling on my plate.

I love you, ice cream, you taste so great!

I love you, Granny – and Grandpa too.

Aren't I lucky that I have you!

I love you, Rabbit. I love you, Ted.

Let's play together

till it's time for bed!

I love you, moon

and stars up above . . .

Oh, the world is full

Of love,

love,

love!